MIRIAM

by
Kjersti Hoff Baez

YOUNG READER'S CHRISTIAN LIBRARY

Illustrations by
Ken Save

A BARBOUR BOOK

Printed in the United States of America
ISBN 1-55748-350-7

95 96 97 5 4 3

MIRIAM

THE MAN FALTERED IN THE MUD

1

"You there!" The overseer's voice ripped through the air. "Get to work!" The slap of a whip crackled and landed cruelly across the shoulders of a tired slave. The man faltered in the mud.

Another Hebrew quickly grabbed his coworker under the arms and steadied him. Satisfied that his victim would continue to work, the taskmaster moved on to another group of men working with the mud of the Nile.

"Are you all right, Simeon?" the man whispered.

"Yes, I'm all right," he answered. "Thanks for helping me, Amram. I'm just so tired today, I guess I'm not really feeling well. But that doesn't mean anything around here, does it?" he said wryly.

Amram wiped the sweat from his brow and shook his head.

"No, I'm afraid not, my friend. There is only one

condition around here for not working—and that's if you're dead!"

The two men laughed sadly and quietly.

The Egyptian sun beat down upon the workers in a torrent of heat. Thousands of slaves labored under the merciless direction of their Egyptian taskmasters.

It was the fall of the year, when the mighty Nile River flooded her banks with life-giving water. Many slaves worked at irrigating the fields with the river water, preparing them for the following season when the planting would begin.

Other workers bent their backs to the task of making bricks. Some men scooped the clay of the Nile into large jugs and carried the pottery jugs to the brick-making site. Other slaves trampled and kneaded the clay with their feet or with hoes. Workers hauled loads of straw and added them to the wet clay. Straw mixed with the clay produced stronger bricks.

A younger man approached Amram and Simeon

STRAW MIXED WITH CLAY PRODUCED STRONGER BRICKS

and stood next to them in the trough. He spoke in whispers while he poured more straw into the muddy clay.

"My father still talks about the days of Joseph! Says our people lived like royalty in Egypt! I find that hard to believe." He shook his head. His eyes took in the sweeping view of human misery as hundreds of men toiled to make bricks for the Pharaoh's many building projects.

"That was a long time ago," sighed Simeon. "Egypt no longer favors us. We are a threat to them."

"Yes," mused Amram. "Seems Pharoah is afraid we'll revolt and take over. So he works us harder, treats us like beasts of burden."

"A threat!" snorted the younger man. "We are no more a threat than a flock of sheep." His dark eyes burned with frustration and anger. "That's what we are—a flock of ragged sheep. What we need is a shepherd, a leader to help us."

Simeon silenced the young man with a warning.

"WHAT WE NEED IS A SHEPHERD!"

"Don't say such things. You'll get yourself killed." His eyes seemed to fade in the gloom of the moment. "There is no such leader, anyway, so why bother talking about it?"

Amram looked thoughtfully at the two men. In his heart stirred the familiar feeling that perhaps there was going to come a day when Israel would be free. But he thought better of sharing it with them. The utter despair written on their faces forbade Amram from offering any hope to them. He saw the foreman approaching and signalled to his companions. The conversation was over.

A scream erupted from the banks of the river, and all heads turned toward the sound. A man carrying a jar of mud had slipped and fallen to the ground, breaking the jar and scattering shards of pottery in the mud.

"You fool!" screamed one of the taskmasters. "Now look what you've done!" Furious, he began to whip the slave. The man's screams seared the air with misery, a misery that echoed in the hearts of

"YOU FOOL! NOW LOOK WHAT YOU'VE DONE!"

those who listened.

Amram and Simeon stood still for a moment, watching helplessly as the life was cruelly drained from the fallen slave.

"Oh, God!" Amram groaned aloud.

A taskmaster standing nearby looked at Amram. He laughed.

"God? You Israelites have a god?" He approached Amram with a grin. Amram could see the man was in the mood to talk.

"Tell me about your god," the man said to Amram. "I know you Hebrews have only one god. Only one?"

Amram nodded silently.

The Egyptian shook his head. "That's a pity! Only one god. Why, we have hundreds! Ours is a grand and glorious tradition crowned of course with the mighty bull Apis, god of the sun."

He sneered at the Hebrew. "I heard you call to your god. A lot of good it did for that fellow," he sneered, looking over at the now still body of the

" TELL ME ABOUT YOUR GOD "

beaten slave.

Amram felt anger beginning to burn in his chest. He began to say something, but Simeon grabbed him by the arm. The Egyptian smiled.

"You have a smart friend. Better not say anything rash. You wouldn't want to make me angry, would you?" He laughed and fingered his whip. "I hear your god is invisible. More's the pity. He must be deaf too! At least we can see our gods! And look at where our gods have gotten us! We rule the earth!" He jabbed a finger in the air and pointed to the dead slave. "Look where your god has gotten you! You are nothing!" He laughed. "Keep crying out to your god if it makes you feel better! He is no threat to us!"

The man swaggered away, cracking his whip into the air. Amram resumed his job of mixing the mud. He looked over at the young man with the straw. His dark eyes smoldered with hurt and anger.

The young man cursed under his breath. "Per-

"LOOK WHERE YOUR GOD HAS GOTTEN YOU!"

haps he is right!" he hissed at Amram. "Where is the God of our fathers now?"

Amram looked heavenward. "I will never lose hope," he answered the young man's despair. "Never."

The door to the clay house swung open with a creak. Amram wearily entered his home and shut the door behind him. A young girl ran up to greet him.

"Father!" she giggled and threw her arms around him.

"Miriam, my little songbird." The man's face brightened with a smile and he momentarily forgot his weariness. "How was your day today?" he asked.

"Fine, Father." Miriam stepped back to smooth down her hair. "Except for Aaron. I had to chase him all afternoon. He wouldn't sit still or stop jabbering for one minute!" She glared at a tall

"MIRIAM, MY LITTLE SONG BIRD"

basket in the corner.

A little three-year-old boy with tangled brown curls peered out from behind the basket. "Aaron good boy?" he chirped, his eyes sending his father a questioning look.

The man laughed, knelt down and held out his arms. Aaron ran to his father, throwing his sister a triumphant smirk.

"I tried to keep him from pestering Mama," the young girl continued. "But it wasn't easy."

The man stood up and looked around the one-room home. "And where is your mother?"

In answer to his question, the door swung open.

"Hello, Amram," a woman's voice rested softly in the air.

"She went to see Shiphrah and Puah," declared Miriam importantly.

"Jochebed?" Amram looked anxiously at his wife.

"Because it's almost time, Mama says."

"Miriam, go get the bread ready for supper," said

"HELLO AMRAM"

Jochebed.

"Your father must be starving."

Jochebed's swelling stomach indeed indicated that the time for the new baby would be soon. Amram helped his wife sit down on the mat in the corner of the room. He could tell by the look on her face that something was wrong. He sat down next to her. Aaron jumped on top of his father and circled his neck with chubby arms.

"Go help your sister, little boy," said Amram. He gently freed himself from the child's grip. "Run along and help her with the bread."

"Bread!" the child echoed eagerly. He ran over to his sister and held onto the folds of her long tunic. "I help. I help," Aaron chattered.

"You can help by keeping quiet," Amram heard Miriam hush her little brother.

Amram smiled and turned his attention to his wife. Her troubled face worried him.

"What is it, Jochebed?" he implored her quietly. "What's wrong?"

"WHAT IS IT, JOCHEBED...WHAT'S WRONG?"

"HE HAS ORDERED THE MIDWIVES TO KILL ALL BABY BOYS"

2

Jochebed tried to get comfortable on the woven mat.

"I went to see the midwives today," she whispered.

"Is there something wrong with the baby?" Amram asked, his voice strained with concern.

"No, no, nothing like that," replied Jochebed. "They said the baby won't come for several weeks yet. But Shiphrah said that the Pharaoh is stirring up trouble for us."

"What do you mean? Isn't he always thinking up new ways to torment us?"

Jochebed put her hand protectively on her stomach. "This is different, Amram." She moved closer to him and whispered in his ear. "He has ordered the midwives to kill all baby boys as they are being born. His orders are to make the births look like stillbirths. But if the child is a girl, they must let the baby live." Tears streamed down her face.

The news took his breath away for a moment. What kind of monster was this Pharaoh? How could he possibly carry out such a horrible plan? Amram made a conscious effort to calm himself. He knew that somehow the Lord would take care of his family.

Amram put his arms protectively around his wife. "Don't be afraid," he said soothingly. "You know God has His hand on our children. All our children." He patted her on the stomach. "Everything will be all right, I just know it."

Jochebed wiped her tears and got up slowly from the mat.

"You're right, Amram," she smiled at her husband. "The Lord will take care of us. He always has."

"Supper's ready!" Miriam called to her parents.

"Sup sup!" squealed Aaron.

The couple joined the two children near the flat

WHAT KIND OF MONSTER WAS THIS PHARAOH?

stone and coals that served as an oven. Miriam served them round bread and a pot of meat.

"She's quite a girl, isn't she!" boasted Amram. He smiled at Miriam. "You are very special to the Lord, just like your mother and her mother before her."

Miriam blushed and handed her little brother a piece of bread.

"Tell me the story of Mother and Grandmother again," she asked her father.

"Again?" Amram asked, with a wink to his wife. "You've heard that story a thousand times!"

"Please," implored Miriam. "You know I love it!"

"Amram, don't tease her. Tell her the story. Only please, eat your dinner before it gets cold!"

He laughed. "Very well. Let's eat!"

After enjoying their simple meal of meat, bread, and leeks, Miriam prompted her father to begin the story. He stoked the fire on the flat rocks of the cooking pit.

...MIRIAM PROMPTED HER FATHER TO BEGIN THE STORY

"Your grandmother Kezia possessed a strong faith in the God of our fathers—"

"Abraham, Isaac, and Jacob!" Miriam piped in.

"Yes," Amram nodded, smiling at his daughter. "Abraham, Isaac, and Jacob. Your grandmother's faith was strong and true. She taught all her children to trust in the Lord, no matter what their circumstances might be. Everyone who knew Kezia would go to her for advice and counsel. She was greatly loved and revered."

The glowing red coals sizzled and sparked as Amram once again poked them with his stick. Miriam stared into the fire, trying to imagine Kezia's home and Kezia's fire. She imagined a cluster of neighbors huddled around the fire, listening to Kezia talk about the Lord.

Amram cleared his throat. "Are you with me, daughter? You look as though you've wandered off!"

"No, I'm listening, Father!" responded Miriam. "Please continue!"

"ARE YOU WITH ME, DAUGHTER?"

Jochebed sighed and shook her head. "You're dragging out the story, my husband. We'll be sitting here all night. Tell it already!" she said with a tired smile.

"Because your grandmother was so faithful, the blessing of God was on her house, even in the land of bondage."

"The land of Pharaoh," said Miriam.

"That's right. Anyway, the Lord blessed Kezia with three sons and two daughters—"

"But then one summer day—" Miriam interrupted.

"One hot summer day, your grandmother was going to give birth to another child. She suddenly became ill and the midwives feared both she and the baby would die. But your grandmother lifted her eyes to heaven and prayed: 'O Glorious Lord, please save me and my child. Let me live to care for my children. I will declare Your wonders to all who will listen.' "

Amram leaned forward for dramatic effect. "Your

"WE'LL BE SITTING HERE ALL NIGHT...TELL IT ALREADY!"

grandmother's face became filled with peace and her eyes sparkled with life. She rested, and the child was born."

"It was a girl!" Miriam fairly squealed.

"That's right!" Amram clapped his hands together. "And they gave the new little baby the name Jochebed, which means...."

"Jehovah is glorious!" Miriam uttered the words in such a lilting voice that it sounded like a song. "That's Mama!"

"Mama, Mama," echoed Aaron, looking curiously around the room. What was all the fuss about?

"In our times, there are very few names linked with the Lord's name." Amram looked at his wife with love in his eyes. "His hand is on your mother. And on you, Miriam, and Aaron, and the child to come." Amram drew a deep breath and looked somewhere beyond the clay bricks of his humble home. "You are special to Him. I believe you will all be special in the lives of our people."

"MAMA, MAMA"

Miriam gazed into her father's face. She loved to hear him talk about the things of the Lord.

Jochebed's voice gently called husband and daughter back to the business at hand. "Yes, yes, now let's clean up and let your father go to sleep. He needs to rest." She shooed the family away from the small stone oven and carefully swept the floor.

Amram lay down on his mat. Miriam took her mat from the corner, unrolled it, and was soon fast asleep herself. Aaron curled up next to his father. After squirming and giggling and pulling his father's beard, Aaron was asleep as well.

Jochebed sat down by herself, staring at the glowing coals and embers of the dying fire. She wrapped her arms around her stomach and whispered a prayer.

"Protect this child," she prayed. "Protect this baby from Pharaoh." The tears on her face glistened in the flickering light.

"Hear my prayer, O Lord. Hear my prayer."

"HEAR MY PRAYER, O LORD. HEAR MY PRAYER"

"PHARAOH HAS LOST HIS MIND"

3

The late night sky glittered overhead with a myriad of stars as Amram made his way through the narrow street of the Hebrew settlement. He watched furtively to see if any Egyptian men were anywhere in the vicinity. His heart pounded with anxiety.

It can't be true, he thought as he approached the home of one of the midwives. *It simply can't be true*. The memory of what had happened earlier that day weighed heavily on his mind.

Amram had been chosen this day to haul the mud from the river. As he filled one of the jugs with the rich clay of the Nile, one of his fellow workers placed his empty pottery close to Amram's jug.

"There's word going around that Pharaoh has lost his mind," the man had whispered urgently to Amram. "He's gone crazy with fear and hatred for our people." The man carefully filled his jug.

"What now?" asked Amram with his eye on the nearest taskmaster.

The man looked into Amram's eyes. "He has commanded his people to take all the male Hebrew babies they can find and throw them into the river." The man had choked on his words. He finished his work and stood up. "I know that your wife is due any time." His eyes were filled with concern. "Perhaps you'll have a girl."

Amram stopped for a moment, trying to shake the memory of the man's eyes out of his head. Underneath the dark Egyptian sky Amram trembled with fear and anger. Gaining control of himself, he quickly approached Puah's home. He knocked quietly on the door.

"Who is it?" A muffled voice responded to the knock. "Who's there?"

"It is Amram, Jochebed's husband," he spoke urgently.

The door swung open and Amram hurried into the home. Puah the midwife was sitting at her fire.

AMRAM TREMBLED WITH FEAR AND ANGER

Her husband pointed to a mat and signalled Amram to sit down.

"So you have heard," said Puah, reading the fear in Amram's face. "Soon all will know." She sighed and fingered her woolen veil. "You know he tried to get us to kill the babies ourselves."

Amram nodded. "You and Shiphrah are very brave women."

Puah pushed away his compliment with a wave of her hand.

"Anyone would have done the same," she said. She sighed at the thought of it. "Pharaoh had wanted us to kill the baby boys before the women knew they were delivered. Clever man, Pharaoh. It would look like a miscarriage, or stillbirth. But we wouldn't do it." Her eyes gleamed. "When Pharaoh called us to court, he asked why there were baby boys among the Hebrews. 'Why have you let the boys live?'" Puah mimicked the Pharaoh's thundering voice. "'Why are you doing this?'"

"...WE WOULDN'T DO IT"

"He was trying to frighten us. But we fear only God." Puah's voice was firm. "We told him Hebrew women are not like the Egyptian women who have long, drawn-out deliveries." She laughed. "We told him the Hebrew women's babies arrive before we get there, and then it's too late. We can't take the babies from the mothers' arms and kill them, can we?" Her voice faded. "He knew we would not do such a thing. So now he has given the job to his own people."

Puah looked at Amram, her almond-shaped eyes smoldering with anger and sadness. "All Hebrew baby boys are to be thrown into the river."

Amram buried his face in his hands. He sobbed openly, his body heaving with grief. In his heart, he just knew the child his wife was carrying was a boy. He just knew it.

Puah's husband put his hand on Amram's shoulder. He didn't know what to say. Puah did not doubt that this man knew the coming baby was a son.

HE SOBBED OPENLY

"We're telling everyone to try to hide their babies," instructed the midwife. "Dress them as girls, hide them in the house, do anything. Perhaps this madness will not last, perhaps God will have mercy and the Egyptians won't have the stomach to keep this murderous plan alive for long. We shall see."

Amram became silent. He stared at the small cooking fire, his tears blurring the colors of the flame into a soft hazy yellow. He felt strangely better, now that he had the news straight from the midwife herself. There was a definite peace in his heart. He decided there was no need to try to understand it. He would simply have to trust God.

"Trust in the Lord," Puah whispered, echoing Amram's unspoken thoughts. "Perhaps He will make a way for your child."

Amram smiled and grasped Puah's hand. "You are right, Puah. He will show us what to do." He rose to his feet. "Thank you both for your concern. The Lord be with you."

"HE WILL SHOW US WHAT TO DO"

As Amram returned outside to the darkened pathways, he had only one question on his mind. *How was he going to tell Jochebed?*

Jochebed wailed and wept at the news. Amram tried to calm her, but he felt totally helpless. She, too, knew in her heart this child to come was a boy. Her heart convulsed with fear.

"God will make a way," was all he could say to her.

Jochebed clung to his words with all her heart.

"GOD WILL MAKE A WAY"

"HE'S QUITE A BABY!"

4

"It's a boy!" Shiphrah whispered excitedly. She held up the wailing newborn to a weary but happy Jochebed.

"He's beautiful." She stared at the baby, her heart warm with love. A pang of fear shot through her mind. Pharaoh. They were killing all the baby boys.

Puah wiped the baby clean and handed him over to his mother. "He's quite a baby!" she said.

Shiphrah nodded in agreement. "And we will keep this to ourselves." She patted Jochebed's hand. "Try not to worry."

Amram stood silently in the corner of the room. His heart was bursting with pride at the sight of his new son. He walked over and gently kissed Jochebed on her forehead.

"Oh, my, we almost forgot about the father!" Puah laughed. "Congratulations, Amram. You have a fine son."

"Thank you," Amram beamed. He took the baby from Jochebed and held him close against his face. "The Lord bless you and keep you," he whispered.

Puah and Shiphrah gathered their things. "We had better get going," said Puah.

"Thank you so much for your help," Jochebed said to the two midwives.

"You're welcome, my dear," clucked Shiphrah. "You get some rest now."

"By the way, what are you going to call him?" inquired Puah.

Amram started to say something, but Jochebed stopped him.

"We are not going to name him right now. The Lord will give him a name." She spoke with firm conviction in her voice.

The midwives and Amram looked at her with questioning glances.

"For now I will call him my son," she said quietly.

"WE ARE NOT GOING TO NAME HIM RIGHT NOW"

"God be with you and the child," the midwives echoed each other and then left as discreetly as possible. Amram returned the baby to the arms of his mother.

"I know the Lord will give him a name," Jochebed explained to her husband. "Just look at him. There is something special about this child." She caressed his tiny little hand. "Something very special."

Amram headed for the door. "I'll go find Miriam and Aaron. They went for a walk. I told them not to go too far."

Soon the door burst open and in hurried Miriam and Aaron. Squeals of delight filled the air as they marvelled at their new baby brother.

"Baby! Baby!" whooped Aaron.

Jochebed pulled Aaron gently to her side. "Shhh, little Aaron. We must be quiet about baby, okay? Can you talk quietly about baby?"

Aaron's eyes grew big and he nodded. "Shhh," he said in hushed tones. "Shhh."

"THERE IS SOMETHING SPECIAL ABOUT THIS CHILD"

Jochebed smiled at him. "Good boy."

She turned toward Miriam. "Remember what we talked about before, Miriam?"

"Yes, Mama. We mustn't let anyone know about our baby boy. We must hide him from Pharaoh and his people."

Amram gave his daughter a hug. "You have a good head on your shoulders, daughter. Just remember, everything will work out fine. The Lord will show us what to do."

"In the meantime," said Jochebed, "we will hide him for as long as we can. I will keep him in the house at all times." She caressed his silken hair. "He is tiny now. It won't be too hard to hide him for a while."

Three months passed quickly. The new baby was growing and Jochebed knew she could no longer hide him in the house safely. A plan had been forming in her mind for several weeks. Now was the time to carry it out.

A PLAN HAD BEEN FORMING IN HER MIND...

Taking papyrus leaves from the banks of the Nile, Jochebed made a basket. She braided the leaves together. Amram brought her a mixture of tar and bitumen. She coated the basket with the mixture to make it waterproof. Miriam watched intently as her mother worked.

"Before the sun rises tomorrow, we will hide the baby in the basket and place it among the reeds in the river," Jochebed explained. "After that, it is up to the Lord to take care of him."

Miriam nodded. She saw the look of faith in her parents' eyes. She walked over and picked up the three-month-old baby. His dark eyes twinkled up at his big sister. The Lord was going to do something special for this special child. Miriam just knew it. Her parents' faith had been planted in her own heart. Her young heart began to pound at the prospect of seeing the Lord at work on their behalf. She gave the baby a warm hug and kissed his soft little face.

HER PARENTS' FAITH HAD BEEN PLANTED IN HER OWN HEART

"...TO HIM I ENTRUST MY SON"

5

Jochebed held her little son in her arms the whole night through. She knew it would probably be the last night she would have to hold him close. As early morning arrived, Amram urged Jochebed to hurry.

"It's time," he said. "You must go while it is still dark." He leaned over and kissed his son good-bye. "God be with you," he said softly.

Miriam followed her mother out the door. They hurried quietly to the path that led to the river. The Nile flowed silently in the fading darkness.

"Well, Nile River," spoke Jochebed to the flowing water, "the Egyptians worship you as a god. But we trust in the God who created you. And it is to Him that I entrust my son."

A faint hint of pink in the eastern sky warned Jochebed that soon the sun would be up. She found the spot on the bank she was looking for.

Saying a quick prayer to the Lord for protection, Jochebed hid the basket in the water among the reeds.

Jochebed hurried away, afraid she might change her mind and take the precious basket home again. Miriam stayed near the basket, hiding herself a few yards away. She wanted to see what the Lord was going to do for her baby brother.

The sky brightened and soon a group of young Egyptian women approached the Nile to pay homage to the river and to bathe in it. To Miriam's surprise, she recognized one of the young women. It was the daughter of Pharaoh!

The princess was dressed in a flowing white tunic. She wore a golden band around her head, and golden bracelets graced her arms. Miriam listened as the women laughed and talked together. She held her breath. They were approaching the bank near the reeds where the basket was hidden!

IT WAS THE DAUGHTER OF PHARAOH!

MIRIAM

Just then, the baby started to cry.

"What was that?" said the young princess. "It sounded like a baby!"

"A baby!" responded one of her companions. "You must be hearing things, Princess Tiya!"

The princess signalled her friends to be still. The baby whimpered.

"There it is again! It surely sounds like a baby crying! It's coming from over there, by those reeds." She pointed in the direction of the basket. Miriam nearly gasped with excitement.

"Go and see what it is," she commanded one of her servant girls.

The servant obeyed and waded in among the reeds. She found the papyrus basket and brought it to the princess. Pharaoh's daughter opened the basket. The baby began to cry in earnest.

"It is a baby!" she exclaimed. "Oh, the poor thing. It's one of the Hebrew babies." She reached into the basket and picked him up. "He certainly is a beautiful child!"

"IT'S ONE OF THE HEBREW BABIES"

MIRIAM

The women all agreed. "But what are you going to do with him, Tiya?" asked Shiptar, the princess's best friend.

As she gazed at the crying little one, the princess's heart warmed with love for him. "I'm going to keep him!" she announced.

"What about your father?" one of the servants reminded her. "It's his command that probably got that baby in the water in the first place!"

Tiya laughed as the baby grabbed her long black hair. "There are other foreigners in the court who are being trained to serve Pharaoh. Why not this little one? Besides, look how wonderful he is." She fingered his soft black hair. "Your mother couldn't bear to see you drowned, could she?" she whispered to the baby. "So she hid you on the river. What a wise mother!" Tiya straightened her hair. "After all, I may never have a child of my own," she said quietly.

Miriam looked on, bursting with excitement. The princess was going to keep the baby!

THE PRINCESS WAS GOING TO KEEP THE BABY!

"Well, I suggest you find a nurse for him," remarked Shiptar, as the baby began to cry harder. "I think he's hungry."

A nurse! Miriam's mind raced with a perfect idea. Quietly coming out from her hiding place, she approached the group of women as if she was just passing by.

"Excuse me," spoke Miriam politely. "I see you have found a Hebrew baby there."

"Yes, we have," retorted one of the servant girls. "And it's none of your business."

Miriam didn't flinch at the servant's rebuke. "It's sounds like the baby needs to be nursed. I think I can help you."

"We'll handle this," snapped the servant.

"Be quiet," commanded Tiya. She studied the young Hebrew girl who stood before her. She looked like an intelligent girl. "What do you suggest, child?"

"I could find a Hebrew woman to nurse the baby for you, if you like."

"WHAT DO YOU SUGGEST, CHILD?"

Tiya nodded. "That is a good idea." She looked down at the squalling infant. "And I think you'd better hurry." The princess took off one of her bracelets with her name engraved on it. "Tell the woman to come right away. If anyone gives her trouble, have her show them my bracelet."

Miriam raced home, clinging to the golden bracelet with all her might. She burst into the room. Jochebed looked up at her with hope in her eyes.

"What happened?" she asked, her voice trembling.

"Mama! The Lord has done a great thing!"

"Speak, child, or I think I'll faint."

"It was the princess who found our baby. Princess Tiya."

Jochebed's eyes widened at the news. The daughter of Sethos? The daughter of Pharaoh? A cold finger of fear gripped her heart. "What—"

"She wants to keep him, Mama. She thinks he's beautiful."

"MAMA! THE LORD HAS DONE A GREAT THING!"

Jochebed's face lit up with joy. "He's safe! And he will be well cared for! The Lord is good!" Tears of happiness streamed down her face.

Mingled with the relief that her child was safe, Jochebed's heart was torn. Her arms felt empty. She longed to scoop her little son in her arms and never let him go again. But he was in the Lord's hands now. She would have to carry him in her heart.

"But Mama, that's not all!" Miriam interrupted her mother's thoughts. "She needs someone to nurse him. I told her I could find someone to nurse the baby." Miriam handed the gold bracelet to her mother. "I've come to get you, Mama. You can nurse the baby."

Jochebed fell to her knees. She wrapped her arms around her daughter. "Miriam, you wonderful, wise little girl! I thought I might never see my son again. The Lord be praised!"

Miriam giggled from within her mother's embrace. "Let me go, Mama. We had better hurry

"MIRIAM, YOU WONDERFUL, WISE LITTLE GIRL!"

back to the princess. The baby is crying a lot."

They left Aaron with a neighbor and rushed to the palace. A wary guard attempted to stop them, but Jochebed held up the princess's bracelet. The guard nodded and a servant took them to the princess's chamber. They could hear the baby from the hallway. Jochebed's heart leaped at the sound of her son's cries.

Miriam stood shyly at the door with her mother. Tiya called them into the room.

"This is Jochebed," said Miriam.

"You have milk for this baby?" Tiya asked.

Jochebed nodded.

The princess commanded one of her servant girls to give the baby to the Hebrew woman. Feeling his mother's touch, the baby calmed down and Jochebed fed him.

Tiya smiled. "I see he responds nicely to you. I would like you to nurse him for me. I will pay you, of course. He is to live with you for the time being. Bring him here every week so I may see how he is

"I WILL PAY YOU, OF COURSE"

doing." She gently stroked his head. The baby had fallen asleep. His black eyelashes fell softly against his cheeks. "I have decided to adopt him as my own son."

"She drew him out of the water," said Miriam.

"Yes," said Tiya. "We drew him out of the water." She stopped for a moment. "That's it!" she laughed. "I've been thinking about a name for him. I like the sound of your Hebrew words for 'drawing out.' I will call him Moses."

"Moses," echoed Jochebed.

"You may go now," said the princess. "By the way, little girl, what is your name?"

"Miriam." The young girl blushed.

"Well, Miriam, you make sure Jochebed brings the baby to me every week so I may see him. You can come too, if you like."

"Oh, thank you, ma'am. I would like that very much."

"Very well. My servant will see you out of the palace."

"MOSES", ECHOED JOCHEBED

Jochebed and Miriam left the palace and hurried toward home. They stopped to pick up Aaron. Finally home, Jochebed shut the door behind her and cradled the baby close to her heart. She closed her eyes and let the tears come. "He is alive, he is safe, and his name is Moses. The Lord has done more than I could ever have hoped for." She looked over at Miriam. Her eyes were shining with joy.

"Just wait until Papa gets home!" said Miriam excitedly.

"Miriam, the Lord's blessing is on you!" Jochebed swept her into a warm hug.

"Mama! Mama!" Aaron screeched with jealousy. He tugged at his mother's robe and tried to pull Miriam away. "Hug Aaron," he whimpered.

Jochebed laughed and cuddled all three children in her arms.

"Children are a gift from God," she said. "You are all my little gifts."

Aaron pinched Miriam. She let out a yell and

SHE CLOSED HER EYES AND LET THE TEARS COME

they were off in a noisy chase around the room. Their mother watched them, savoring every squeal and snatch of laughter.

THEY WERE OFF IN A NOISY CHASE AROUND THE ROOM

LITTLE MOSES GREW QUICKLY

6

Little Moses grew quickly and at the age of three he no longer needed to be nursed. Miriam helped her mother pack his clothes and get him ready to move to the palace. Jochebed hummed as she folded the garments the princess had given to Moses.

Amram held his son above his head, making him giggle with delight. Jochebed looked over at them and smiled.

"This is a happy day for us," she remarked. "Even though our Moses is going to live with the princess, we must remember how God has preserved his life."

Amram nodded and tickled his youngest son. "The plan of the Lord continues to unfold," he said. "And I'm sure there is more to come."

Miriam sat quietly in the corner and watched the happy scene. She felt a tinge of sadness that little

Moses was moving out. She would miss seeing him every day. Sitting there, Miriam made a promise to herself and her mother. For as long as she lived, Miriam would keep an eye on her brother Moses.

"The princess says I can come and play with Moses whenever I want," Miriam reminded her parents. "And she said I could take him out for walks if I wanted to."

"Bring him here to play with me," demanded six-year-old Aaron. "I am his big brother, you know."

Jochebed laughed. "Honestly, Aaron, the way you stick to Moses I sometimes think you two are sewn together like two garments."

"May they always stick together," prayed Amram with a laugh.

"Amen," responded Jochebed.

"Amen," giggled little Moses.

Miriam laughed and grabbed her two brothers in a sisterly hug. "We'll all stick together!" she exclaimed.

"MAY THEY ALWAYS STICK TOGETHER"

MIRIAM

The years flew by as steadily as the Nile. Moses was trained and educated in the Egyptian courts. Princess Tiya never knew that Miriam was really Moses' sister. Miriam came to see him and he often visited his Hebrew family. Amram continued to work beneath the fury of the sun and the taskmasters of Egypt. When Aaron was old enough, he joined his father in the grueling work.

The day came when Amram could no longer endure the hardship. He came down with a fever and lay on his mat, unable to get up. Jochebed and Miriam stayed by his side, praying he would not suffer long.

Amram's face was pale in the flickering light of the family's oil lamp. Despite his struggle to breathe, there was a determination in his eyes.

"Never forget what the Lord has promised," he said to his wife and daughter. "There will come deliverance for our people from this land of bondage. Never lose hope." He smiled up at them and breathed his last breath.

MOSES WAS TRAINED AND EDUCATED IN THE EGYPTIAN COURTS

Jochebed turned to her daughter. "Go and tell Moses and Aaron what has happened. Tell them that the tyranny of Egypt has finally claimed the life of their father."

Out in the work fields Miriam searched for Aaron. She found him near the river gathering clay. His eyes brimmed with sorrow at the news of Amram's death.

"At least now he can rest," said Aaron, as he scooped up the clay and put it in his jug. He looked at Miriam. "You'd better go before—"

"Get out of there, woman!" The voice of a taskmaster boomed. "Get out before I use my whip to persuade you!"

Miriam hurried away and headed for the palace.

At the palace, Miriam spoke to Moses privately about his father. No one in the courts was aware that Moses knew who his real parents were. Now the young prince of Egypt groaned with sorrow. He clenched his fist in anger and frustration.

"What can be done?" he asked Miriam. "What

THE YOUNG PRINCE OF EGYPT GROANED WITH SORROW

can be done to help our people?"

"Only the Lord knows the answer to that," replied Miriam. "Only He can make a way."

"And who is the Lord?" asked Moses, half to himself.

"Don't let the teachings of the Egyptian court cloud your memory, my brother." Miriam reprimanded him. "Remember what our parents taught us about the God of our fathers."

Moses said nothing. He looked out at the impressive buildings of Pharaoh's court. "Built by the sweat and blood of my people," he said. "If only something could be done."

Miriam could see that her brother needed to be alone, so she left him and returned home to comfort her mother.

Several days later there was an urgent knocking at the door of Jochebed's home. Miriam and Jochebed looked up as their neighbor flew into the house with a frantic look on her face.

"Rachel, what's wrong?" Jochebed asked. "You

...HER BROTHER NEEDED TO BE ALONE.

look terrible."

The woman grabbed Jochebed by the arms. "It's Moses!" she whispered hoarsely. "The news is spreading like wild fire all over the work fields." She paused to catch her breath.

"What? What happened to Moses?" demanded Jochebed.

"He killed an Egyptian!" Rachel hissed. "In broad daylight! He killed an Egyptian!"

Jochebed closed her eyes and sunk to her knees. "Oh, no." Miriam put her arms around her mother.

"Moses saw one of our men being beaten by this Egyptian overseer," Rachel explained. "Moses apparently thought no one was looking; he came to the slave's rescue and killed the Egyptian. Well," she continued, taking a breath, "the next day, Moses saw a Hebrew beating up another Hebrew. He asked the man why he would treat a fellow Hebrew that way and the man told Moses he wasn't ruler and judge. Then the man asked Moses if he was going to kill him like he killed the

"HE KILLED AN EGYPTIAN!"

Egyptian."

Miriam shook her head. "If our people know about this, it's only a matter of time before Pharaoh hears of it. He will be furious. Moses will be in great danger."

"That's for sure," Rachel said firmly. "Pharaoh won't let him get away with that, even though he is considered Tiya's son."

When evening came and cloaked the land with darkness, the door to Jochebed's home was quietly opened. Aaron stepped in from the shadows.

"He's gone," said Aaron.

Jochebed sighed with relief. "Moses has fled Egypt? Do you think he got away safely?"

"Yes," replied Aaron. He leaned close to his mother and spoke in a whisper. "He told me he was going to Midian. It's far away and no one will know him there."

Jochebed sat back on her mat. "The Lord saved Moses from Pharaoh when he was a baby. The

"HE TOLD ME HE WAS GOING TO MIDIAN"

Lord has saved his life again." She looked up at Aaron. "I know I will not see Moses again. But I know the Lord's plan will not be thwarted. Pharaoh cannot get in the way of God."

Miriam sat quietly listening to her mother's words.

I wonder if I will see Moses again? she thought to herself. Deep in her heart she sensed the answer. Somehow, some way, in God's time, Moses would return to Egypt.

...IN GOD'S TIME, MOSES WOULD RETURN TO EGYPT

RAMSES II BECAME THE NEW RULER OF EGYPT

7

Miriam married and had a family of her own. Jochebed passed away, her faith still bright in her heart. Aaron married and his wife gave him four sons. Forty years passed, each year bringing more misery for the Hebrew slaves in Egypt. Finally, Sethos the Pharaoh died. However, his death did not bring relief to the slaves. Ramses II became the new ruler of Egypt. More stubborn and heartless than the Pharaoh before him, Ramses burdened the slaves with more work, more cruelty.

Miriam worked in the fields, planting and harvesting. The seemingly endless work and hardship droned on through the years. For Miriam, flashes of hope sometimes interrupted the bleak rhythm of bondage. Thoughts of Moses would come to her, thoughts of what her father had said. Sometimes at night his words would come to her, ringing in her mind like a beautiful song. Sometimes during the day when she bent her back to bring in the harvest for Pharaoh, Amram's words would come singing into her heart. Amid the sounds of the weeping of a weary slave, the moaning of the dying, on the banks of the Nile, the words would come. "His hand is on your mother. And on you and Aaron and Moses. You are special to Him. I believe you will all be special in the lives of our people." Her father's words flashed like light in the darkness, and then Miriam would remember her mother's words. "The plan of the Lord will not be thwarted. Pharaoh cannot get in the way of God."

One night Miriam stood at the door of her house, looking out at the dismal neighborhood of her fellow Hebrews. The muffled sound of a baby's cry rested pitifully in the night air. Miriam knew that more and more of her people were reaching their limits. They could no longer cope with the heartaches of bondage. More and more people were crying out for help. Suddenly, Miriam felt as

...MIRIAM WOULD REMEMBER HER MOTHER'S WORDS

though she could hear the cries of her people rising in the night air, rising up and reaching the ears of God.

Little did they know that God had heard their cry. Help was on the way.

"I must go to the desert and meet with Moses," Aaron spoke urgently with Miriam.

Miriam looked into her brother's eyes. Something had happened to him. "What are you saying, Aaron? I don't understand."

Aaron took his sister by the hand. "The Lord spoke to me last night. He said I must go to the desert to see Moses. He said I must go to Mount Horeb, that I will meet Moses there."

Miriam caught her breath. "Aaron! Do you realize what this means? The Lord has heard our prayers. The Lord is going to keep His promise. Father was right! God is going to do something for the children of Israel! Oh, I could sing at the top

"AARON! DO YOU REALIZE WHAT THIS MEANS?"

of my voice!"

Aaron smiled and squeezed Miriam's hand. "Sing to the Lord all you want, dear sister. The Lord is faithful! And while you're at it, pray. I'm leaving tonight for the desert."

Miriam nodded and bade her brother a good journey. After he left, Miriam sang a song of thanks to the Lord. Then she whispered a prayer. "After forty long years, O Lord, you have heard our cries for help. May You come and deliver us from this house of bondage."

Several weeks of waiting were rewarded one night with a knock at the door. In stepped Aaron and Moses. Miriam looked at her brothers in awed silence. She was beginning to see the hand of God at work.

"I found him at Mount Horeb, just as the Lord had said," spoke Aaron. "And he has told me all that the Lord has instructed him."

Miriam looked at Moses' face. There was something different about her youngest brother, some-

IN STEPPED AARON AND MOSES

thing in his eyes. Her mind flashed back to the baby in the basket, hidden in the Nile. She remembered the young man, frustrated and angry over the death of his father. Who was this Moses who stood before her now? This man had a look of purpose in his eyes. What had happened to him, what had changed his life?

"I have been with the Lord," Moses said quietly. "The God of our fathers, Abraham, Isaac, and Jacob. He said His name is 'I am.' The Lord!"

Miriam fell to her knees at the awesome words. Moses joined her on his knees. "He has sent me to bring our people out of Egypt."

Miriam's eyes widened and brimmed over with tears. "May the Lord be with you, my brother. I will stand by you and pray for you always."

"You have always been a good sister," Moses smiled. "And Aaron is to work with me. He will speak whatever the Lord tells me to say. He always was a better speaker than I!" Moses smiled at his brother. Aaron couldn't say anything. He

"I HAVE BEEN WITH THE LORD"

was overwhelmed with the wonder of the moment.
Moses laughed. "You'll have to do better than
that, my brother!"

Miriam prepared a meal for them. Aaron explained what the Lord had commanded them to do.
"We are meeting with the elders of Israel tonight,
to tell them what the Lord is doing. And tomorrow
we go to Pharaoh."

They left and called together the elders. Aaron
explained to the elders everything the Lord had
told Moses. Then the elders summoned the people
together.

"The Lord has sent this man Moses to us, to bring
us out of Egypt," one of the elders announced to
the crowds.

The people looked at Moses. They saw a quiet,
humble man standing before them. How could he
bring deliverance to them?

"See now that the Lord is with Moses, and that
the Lord has sent him," spoke Aaron.

THE PEOPLE LOOKED AT MOSES

Moses stepped forward. Miriam stood nearby, watching and wondering what Moses was going to do. Moses held up the wooden staff he held in his hand.

"That's just a stick!" someone yelled from the crowd. "Will Moses deliver us from Pharaoh with a stick?"

Moses threw the stick to the ground and it immediately turned into a snake. The crowd stepped back, startled by the miracle. Miriam gasped in wonder as Moses picked up the snake by the tail, returning it to the form of the staff.

"This is the first sign that God has sent Moses," said Aaron.

Then Moses put his hand inside his cloak. When he pulled his hand out again and held it up before the people, it was white with leprosy. Once again the crowd was amazed. Miriam felt a twinge of horror as she looked at the leprous hand. Then Moses put his hand back into his cloak. When he pulled it out again, his hand was restored to health.

...IT IMMEDIATELY TURNED INTO A SNAKE

Lastly, Aaron handed Moses a bowl filled with water.

"Behold the water of the Nile," announced Aaron.

Moses poured the water on the ground. It turned into blood.

"The Lord is surely with us!" exclaimed the people. "He has heard our cries. He cares about us!" Their words mingled in a symphony of worship. Together they all bowed down and worshipped the Lord. Miriam's heart glowed with pure joy as she knelt to worship God.

"THE LORD IS SURELY WITH US!"

"I WILL NOT LET ISRAEL GO!"

8

The morning sun glittered in the sky above as Moses and Aaron made their way to the court of Pharaoh. The people followed them in expectation. As Miriam walked with her neighbors, she prayed earnestly that all would go well.

Moses and Aaron stood before Pharaoh.

"The God of Israel has commanded us to journey to the desert and make sacrifices to Him. He says, O Pharaoh, that you are to let Israel leave Egypt."

Pharaoh laughed at such a preposterous idea.

"And who is this god of whom you speak? I am not familiar with him. Why should I obey him?" He shook his head. The golden headdress Pharaoh wore gleamed in the morning light. "I will not let Israel go. Forget it."

"But the God of the Hebrews has met with us. Let us go and do as He says," Aaron spoke urgently.

Pharaoh looked with disgust at the two men.

"Moses and Aaron! Why are you keeping the people from doing their work?" He looked over at the crowds of people that had gathered there. "Look at this! Thousands of people standing around doing nothing! Get back to your work!" he commanded. "Get back to your work now!"

The people hurried away in shock. What had gone wrong? Why didn't Moses show Pharaoh the power of the Lord? Miriam tried to encourage her friends and neighbors as they all left Pharaoh's palace.

"Don't give up!" she pleaded. "The Lord will work this out!"

But the people shook their heads and returned to their jobs in Pharaoh's fields.

Pharaoh called together all the taskmasters and slave drivers. He commanded them to withhold straw from the Hebrews.

"Do not give them any straw for the bricks. Tell them they must gather the straw themselves. And

"DO NOT GIVE THEM ANY STRAW FOR BRICKS"

I expect them to keep up with the usual quota of bricks I require. Obviously they have too much time on their hands. They are lazy. Give them more work to do! Then they won't have time to listen to the lies this Moses is peddling."

When the Hebrews found out they were to gather their own straw, their hearts sank with despair. It was time consuming. They scattered throughout the land of Egypt picking up the stubble left in the fields. It was impossible to produce the required amount of bricks in one day. When the taskmasters found the number of bricks reduced, they beat the Hebrew foremen.

The foremen went before Pharaoh, bruised and bewildered.

"Why are you not supplying us with straw?" they asked their ruler. "We can't possibly keep up with the quotas if your men don't supply us with straw."

Pharaoh stood with his arms folded across his chest.

"You are lazy people! You say you want to go

THEY BEAT THE HEBREW FOREMEN

to the desert and worship your god, but what you really want is to get a break from working. Get back to work! And find your own straw."

The foremen turned and walked away, shaking their heads in hopelessness.

"And fill your quotas!" the Pharaoh yelled after them.

Moses and Aaron stood waiting outside for the foremen.

"The Lord judge you both!" one of the men said. "Because of you, we are like a bad smell in Pharaoh's nose. He will destroy us! And it is you who put the sword in his hand!"

They turned away from Moses and Aaron with disgust.

Aaron looked at his brother. Moses' face was lined with sadness. His heart ached for his people. Moses walked quickly away and found a place to pray.

"Oh Lord!" Moses prayed. "Why have you done

"THE LORD JUDGE YOU BOTH!"

this to your people? You have not delivered Your people. You have made things worse for them. Why did You send me?"

Moses listened for the Lord's answer. "Now is the time you will see what I will do to Pharaoh. I will deliver Israel with a mighty hand. I will rescue them from their slavery and you will know that I am the Lord your God. I will bring you to the land I gave to Abraham, Isaac, and Jacob. I am the Lord."

A crowd of people crowded into Miriam's house, telling her the news about the straw and the foremen.

"Why is your brother stirring up trouble for us?" one man demanded. "Tell him to go back where he came from!"

"Haven't we suffered enough?" Miriam's friend Rachel asked.

Miriam tried to calm everyone down. "Pharaoh is no match for the Lord," she said earnestly. "Can't you see that God is with Moses? Remem-

"PHARAOH IS NO MATCH FOR THE LORD"

ber the miracles the Lord showed us through Moses?"

"Who cares about a handful of miracles?" sniffed one old man. "Pharaoh didn't seem too impressed with your Moses. He certainly didn't let us go free!"

The crowd murmured in agreement. At that moment Moses and Aaron arrived at the door. The crowd continued to murmur against him.

"Please, hear what the Lord has spoken to Moses," Aaron pleaded.

The crowd got quiet and Moses shared with them what the Lord had told him. "The Lord is going to raise a mighty hand and deliver us from Pharaoh," he said.

The people shook their heads in disbelief. "You have only managed to discourage us even more than before, when we had no hope. We will never be free."

After the people left, Miriam urged Moses and Aaron not to be discouraged. "The Lord is with

"WE WILL NEVER BE FREE"

you!" she said.

"Tomorrow I must go to Pharaoh and tell him to let the people go. He said to perform the miracles before Pharaoh. But if my own people won't listen to me, why should Pharaoh?"

Miriam smiled and said nothing. She knew the Lord was going to do something amazing through Moses.

MIRIAM SMILED AND SAID NOTHING

"I'M SURE MY WISE MEN CAN DO THE SAME

9

"Prove it!" thundered Pharaoh from his throne. "If your god is so mighty and you say he is with you, then prove it."

Pharaoh's officials hovered nearby like royal bees, their voices buzzing in agreement.

Moses looked at Aaron. "Throw down your staff."

Aaron threw his staff to the ground in front of Pharaoh's throne. It immediately became a cobra.

Pharaoh laughed. "I'm sure my wise men can do the same!" He clapped his hands together and summoned his magicians and sorcerers.

Pharaoh's wise men hurried into the room. Pharaoh pointed to the cobra slithering on the floor. "That used to be Aaron's rod. Now you do the same, and show this Moses he is not so powerful!"

The magicians nodded and began to mutter their secret incantations. With quick movements of their hands, they threw their staffs to the ground. Each staff became a snake.

Pharaoh crossed his arms across his chest. "Well, Moses, what can you say to that? You are not the only one who can turn staffs into snakes!" He started laughing. His officials joined in. But suddenly the laughter stopped. Aaron's snake swallowed all the other snakes.

"Oh, no!" yelped one of the startled magicians.

"Silence!" Pharaoh's lips tightened in anger. "Get out!" he commanded Moses. "I'll not listen to any more of your foolishness. I will not let your people go."

Moses turned in silence and left Pharaoh's court. He returned to Goshen, where all the Hebrews lived. Aaron hurried to Miriam's house.

"Tell all your friends to gather extra water for themselves," he said. "Tomorrow the Lord is going to turn the Nile River into blood."

Miriam gasped. "The Nile? Into blood? That will surely show Pharaoh and his people that the

"GET OUT ... I WILL NOT LET YOUR PEOPLE GO!"

Lord is with us!"

She hastened to tell all who would listen to gather water for themselves. The next morning, Moses met Pharaoh at the river.

One of Pharaoh's attendants barred Moses from getting near the Pharaoh. "He is paying homage to the river god Hapi. You must not interrupt him."

When Pharaoh finished worshipping, he turned to leave. There stood Moses.

"The Lord God of the Hebrews has sent me to tell you: 'Let my people go.' But you would not listen. Therefore, I will strike the Nile with my staff, and it shall turn into blood. Then you will know that He is the Lord."

Aaron took the rod and at Moses' command struck the water of the Nile. Before their very eyes, the Nile turned to blood. The fish died and the stench of the Nile was overwhelming. However, the Hebrews in Goshen miraculously had all the water they needed. God was taking care of His people.

"THE NILE ... SHALL TURN INTO BLOOD"

For seven days the river ran red. Moses approached Pharaoh again and warned him that the Lord was going to visit yet another plague on the land of Egypt.

"Frogs will come forth out of the river that you worship. Frogs will cover the land," Moses declared.

Pharaoh refused to listen to Moses. Moses told Aaron to stretch out his staff over the waters of Egypt. As Aaron raised up his staff, frogs by the hundreds came clambering out of the Nile. Streams, canals, and ponds all over Egypt spilled over with frogs. The slimy green amphibians hopped and jumped their way into the homes of the Egyptians. They invaded bedrooms and kitchens, taking over beds and even ovens. All over Egypt the people tried in vain to get the frogs out of their homes. But for every frog they threw out the front door, another came hopping inside.

Pharaoh summoned his magicians.

"Can you call forth frogs, just as Moses did?"

THEY INVADED BEDROOMS AND KITCHENS

demanded the ruler of Egypt.

"Yes, your excellency," the magicians and sorcerers replied.

Wailing and moaning their incantations, they called forth frogs and frogs appeared.

"It's nothing more than a magician's trick," mused Pharaoh. "Moses is nothing more than a clever magician."

"Even so, your highness," said one of Pharaoh's officials cautiously, "we can't rid the land of the frogs. They just keep multiplying. Unless something is done soon, I fear our land is in danger of being destroyed by these frogs."

Pharaoh frowned and called for Moses to come to the palace.

"If you pray to your god to remove the frogs, I will let your people go to the desert and worship their god."

Moses looked at Pharaoh. "I will give you the honor of choosing what time you want me to pray for the frogs to be removed from your homes."

"...WE CAN'T RID THE LAND OF THE FROGS"

"Tomorrow," replied Pharaoh.

"Tomorrow it will be so," said Moses, "and by this you will know that there is no god anywhere like the Lord our God."

The next morning, the Lord responded to Moses' prayer. The frogs all over Egypt began to die, leaving live frogs only in the Nile. The heat from the sun poured down on the frog carcasses, causing them to rot. The smell filled the air with sickening intensity. There were so many dead frogs they had to be thrown into piles throughout Egypt.

Once the frogs were no longer a problem, Pharaoh sent word to Moses that he had changed his mind. He would not let Israel leave.

Moses instructed Aaron to raise his staff again. As Aaron struck the ground, the abundant dust of Egypt became gnats. Tiny insects by the millions swarmed the lands, clinging to people and animals.

THE ABUNDANT DUST OF EGYPT BECAME GNATS

Pharaoh's magicians tried to produce gnats. They failed.

"We can't bring forth gnats," they told Pharaoh. "The finger of God has done this thing to Egypt. Perhaps you had better do what Moses has asked for."

Pharaoh gritted his teeth. "I will not be pushed around by the son of a slave. Get out of my sight!" he shouted at his magicians. "You are useless!"

The plague of the gnats passed. Pharaoh approached the Nile for his daily worship ritual. He looked up and there stood Moses again.

"The Lord says, 'If you don't let the Lord's people go, tomorrow swarms of flies will cover the land of the Egyptians. But you will see that the flies will not go near the land of Goshen. My people will not be afflicted. By this you will know that I am surely with my people.'"

Moses left Pharaoh and returned to Goshen. Miriam greeted Moses at her door.

"Has Pharaoh yielded to the Lord yet?" she

...THERE STOOD MOSES AGAIN

asked.

Moses shook his head sadly. "He is a hard man. He doesn't seem to care about his own land and his own people. Each plague from the Lord is more severe than the one before. He is hurting his own people by refusing to listen to the Lord."

"How long do you think this will go on?" Miriam searched Moses' face for an answer.

Her brother sighed. "I don't know. Only the Lord knows. But rest assured, our deliverance will come. The Lord will bring us out of Egypt with a mighty hand."

Miriam smiled, remembering her father and mother's faith. "The Lord is faithful!"

The following morning Miriam woke to hear a strange sound outside her home. A tremendous buzzing and humming filled the air. She hurried out the door and looked toward the Egyptians' land. She gasped at the sight. Millions of flies hovered in the air, pulsing in the sky, a horrible

"HOW LONG DO YOU THINK THIS WILL GO ON?"

wave of winged misery. They attacked the Egyptians, biting them and infesting their homes and animals. All of Egypt was devastated by the flies.

Miriam surveyed the land of Goshen, her heart pounding. Not one fly flew over the boundary that separated the Egyptian and Hebrew homes. Tears streamed down her face. The vivid picture before her eyes spoke clearly that the Lord was working on behalf of His people. She quietly sang a song about the Creator reaching down and directing His creation for the sake of His people Israel.

Once again, Pharaoh entreated Moses to get rid of this latest plague. Moses prayed to the Lord and the flies were gone. Once again Pharaoh went back on his word.

The next problem to befall Egypt was a plague on the livestock. All the Egyptians' camels, sheep, cattle, and donkeys that were out in the field died mysteriously. Pharaoh sent servants to check on the livestock of the Hebrews. As he suspected, not one of their animals had been afflicted. Still,

SHE QUIETLY SANG A SONG

Pharaoh hardened his heart. He would not let the Israelites leave.

The plagues continued. Moses threw handfuls of ashes in the air. A fine layer of black dust covered the land of Egypt. The skin of man and animal alike became covered with blistering sores. Pharaoh's magicians bent over in agony because of the sores on their bodies. They could not stand before Moses. But Pharaoh stood firm against Moses and his God.

THEY COULD NOT STAND BEFORE MOSES

"IT IS NOT THE POWER OF GOD!"

10

"Hurry, hurry!" Akkad, one of Pharaoh's magicians frantically called to his servants. "Get all my livestock into the shelters. And bring in all my slaves from the fields!"

"Why?" the servant asked in bewilderment.

"Because the God of the Hebrews is going to send a hailstorm on our land. He says it will be the worst hailstorm we have ever seen! Now hurry!"

Akkad and other officials who had learned to take Moses and his God at his word gathered in all their slaves and livestock. Those who did not fear the word of the Lord laughed at Akkad and his fellow magicians.

"Fools!" they snorted. "All this is as Pharaoh said. These plagues are simply coincidences! Natural disasters. It is not the power of God!"

The hailstorm came, ferocious and powerful. Thunder ripped through the air with a deafening roar. Lightning struck the ground with relentless flashes of light. Any living thing in the fields was struck down. Only the crops that had not matured survived. The land of Egypt was ravaged by the storm. At Pharaoh's request Moses prayed for the storm to stop. Yet when the hail and thunder faded away, Pharaoh again hardened his heart against Moses and his God.

"Because you refuse to humble yourself before the Lord, He will send locusts into your land," said Moses. "There will be a whole army of locusts, the likes of which you and your fathers have never seen before."

Pharaoh said nothing as Moses walked away.

Pharaoh's officials gathered around their ruler, pleading for the life of Egypt. "Let this man Moses take his people and go!" they cried earnestly. "Can't you see that our land is ruined because of them? For the sake of Egypt, let the Hebrews go!"

But Pharaoh stood his ground.

THE LAND OF EGYPT WAS RAVAGED BY THE STORM

With each passing plague, excitement stirred in the Hebrew camp. Miriam continued to encourage the people to keep their eyes on the Lord. One morning as she stood with her neighbors discussing the Lord's hand in Egypt, a wind began to blow. It felt warm against Miriam's face.

"An east wind," stated one of the men.

"I wonder what the Lord is doing now?" said Miriam. "I wonder how long Pharaoh is going to hold out?"

The wind blew continuously through the day and night. In the morning, riding on the wind, were millions of locusts. The humming of their wings could be heard for miles. As they landed, they completely covered the ground. Egypt was black with locusts. In a matter of hours the insects devoured every plant and leaf in Egypt.

Moses was immediately summoned to the palace.

"I have sinned against the Lord and against you," said Pharaoh. His officials nodded with

"I HAVE SINNED AGAINST THE LORD AND AGAINST YOU"

relief. At last their leader was going to solve Egypt's current problems.

"Forgive me," continued Pharaoh, "and pray to the Lord. Ask Him to get rid of the locusts."

Moses left Pharaoh and did as he requested. The Lord sent a strong west wind which swept the locusts away into the Red Sea.

As he looked out a palace window and saw that the locusts were gone, a grim smile crossed Pharaoh's face. "You're not going anywhere, Moses!" he said aloud. Pharaoh's officials shook their heads in disbelief. What would happen next in Egypt?

Moses stretched out his hand to the sky. Darkness fell on Egypt, a darkness so deep it could be felt. It obscured the land and permeated the houses. It quenched even the light of a lamp. For three days the Egyptians could not see one another. They stayed inside their homes, trembling with wonder and fear.

DARKNESS FELL ON EGYPT

Miriam looked in amazement at the darkness clouding Egypt. In Goshen, there was no darkness. The boundary between the darkness of Egypt and the light of Goshen was astounding.

"Surely the sun god of Egypt has been stripped of his power!" she said earnestly. "Can't Pharaoh see that his gods are nothing? The Lord has power over the sun! He is the One to be feared and worshipped!"

Pharaoh summoned Moses one more time, and one more time he hardened his heart against the Lord.

"Don't you ever come before me again!" spoke Pharaoh angrily. "If I ever see you again, I will have you killed!"

Moses calmly nodded at Pharaoh's words.

"You are right," Moses said quietly. "I will not see your face ever again." Moses looked straight into Pharaoh's eyes. "At midnight, every firstborn son in Egypt will die, from the firstborn of Pharaoh who sits on his throne, to the firstborn of

"... EVERY FIRST BORN SON IN EGYPT WILL DIE"

the slave girl grinding grain at her mill. Even the firstborn of your beasts will die. There will be weeping and wailing throughout the land, but in Goshen there will be silence. You will see that the Lord is with His people Israel." Moses pointed at the officials of Pharaoh. His voice rose in anger at the stubbornness of Pharaoh. "And these your servants will come and bow down before me, saying, 'Get out, you and all your people!' After that, I will leave this land."

Pharaoh's court was silent as Moses left them.

The Lord had instructed Moses to tell the people to kill a lamb and place the blood on the top and sides of their doorways. This would be a sign of protection for the Hebrews. When the plague of death came, it would not enter the houses sprinkled with blood but would "pass over" them.

Miriam hurried to prepare the "Passover" lamb for her family. Dipping a bunch of hyssop in the basin that held the blood, Miriam wiped it on the

...A SIGN OF PROTECTION FOR THE HEBREWS

top and sides of her doorway. She prepared the meal as the Lord had instructed.

"We are to stay inside our houses," Miriam explained. "And we are not to wait for our bread to rise. There will be no time for that. We must eat our bread flat. And we are to keep our shoes on tonight," continued Miriam, her face glowing, "because tomorrow we will be leaving in a hurry."

All of Israel waited silently in their homes as the night fell on Egypt. Each Hebrew family partook of their Passover meal. Suddenly, a scream pierced the night air.

"It has begun," spoke Miriam. "The firstborn sons of Egypt are being struck down by the plague of death."

Soon the air was filled with wailing and screaming, as Egyptian men and women discovered that their firstborn sons were dead. Their anguish and horror chilled the air with sorrow. Pharaoh looked upon the body of his grown son, heir to the throne. For the moment, his hardened heart broke. He sent

"IT HAS BEGUN"

for his messenger.

"Go quickly," he commanded. "Go to Moses and tell him to leave. Tell him to go, and take all the Israelites, and all their flocks and herds. And ask him for a blessing."

The messenger hurried off into the night with the urgent news. Soon all of Egypt, including Pharaoh's officials, were urging the Hebrews to leave. "Leave us!" they pleaded. "Or perhaps we will all fall from this plague of death."

The Hebrews hurriedly placed their unleavened bread in their kneading troughs. As they left their homes, they followed Moses' instructions and asked their Egyptian neighbors for gold and silver and clothes. The Egyptian people gladly fulfilled the Hebrews' requests. They were in awe of this people whose God was so powerful, a God who came to bring His people out of Egypt. For four hundred and thirty years, Israel had lived in Egypt. Now they journeyed out into the night, free.

Israel marched out of Egypt, grouped according

ISRAEL MARCHED OUT OF EGYPT

to their clans. There were six hundred thousand
men, plus women and children. Other people who
had taken refuge in the homes and faith of the
Hebrews also left with them. Miriam walked with
her family, following those of the clan of Levi. Her
joy increased with each step she took. Her heart
sang with the thought that God had indeed come
and saved His people. No more would they be
slaves to the cruel taskmasters of Egypt. As
Miriam's feet crossed the borders of Egypt, and
entered the desert wilderness, she wept with happiness. All of Israel looked up with wonder as a
huge pillar of fire descended and went before
them.

"The Lord goes before us!" the people shouted.

God led people down the desert road toward the
Red Sea. As the sun began to rise, Miriam watched
a pillar of cloud descend and go before Israel. By
day, the Lord led Israel by the pillar of cloud. At
night, the pillar of fire illumined the darkness with
glorious light. Because of the pillar of cloud and

... A HUGE PILLAR OF FIRE DESCENDED

the pillar of fire, the Hebrews could travel at any time, day or night.

One of Miriam's grandsons looked up at his grandmother, his eyes big with questions. "Where are we going, Grandma?"

Miriam smiled and took the little boy's hand into her own.

"We're going home," she said, her eyes shining with inexpressible joy. "The Lord is leading us home!"

"WE'RE GOING HOME"

"WHAT DO YOU MEAN, 'THEY'RE GONE?'"

11

"They are gone, sir," the messenger bowed before his ruler.

Pharaoh turned swiftly and studied his messenger's face.

"What do you mean, 'They're gone?' " he demanded.

"The Israelites, sir. You told me to tell Moses and his people to leave, and now they are gone."

"All of them?" asked Pharaoh.

The messenger looked puzzled. "Yes, sir. All of them. Just as you commanded."

Pharaoh's face turned red with rage. "Why did we ever let them go?" He looked in anger at his officials. "Now we don't have them here to work for us!"

Pharaoh's officials nodded in agreement. Perhaps they had been too hasty to let the Hebrews go.

Leaping from his throne, the ruler began barking

out orders.

"Get my chariot ready. Order my army to stand ready to march. Send for every chariot in Egypt! We are going after the Israelites! I'll bring them back here if it's the last thing I do!"

Pharaoh rallied his troops and gave the command to pursue. They stormed out of Egypt to follow the trail of the Israelites. The ruler turned his back on his country, leaving it behind in a trail of dust. Amid the flurry of activity, there could still be heard the piercing sound of wailing, as Pharaoh's people wept for their firstborn sons.

The Israelites camped on a peninsula that jutted into the Red Sea. Suddenly a rumbling sound could be heard in the distance.

In the camp, someone called out, "What is that?"

The people looked up and to their horror, the army of Pharaoh loomed on the desert road. The dust from their rapid pursuit flew into the air, heralding the coming of the cruel Pharaoh and his

THE ARMY OF PHARAOH LOOMED ON THE DESERT ROAD

men.

The people ran to Moses, panic-stricken. "Why did you take us out of Egypt? So we could die here in the wilderness? We told you to leave us alone, didn't we? It would be better to serve the Egyptians and be alive, than to die here in the desert!"

Moses looked with understanding into the faces of the frightened people. Israel was trapped on the peninsula, hemmed in by the sea. It seemed there was no way out.

"Don't be afraid. Stand still and watch the Lord deliver you today. The Egyptians you see this day you will never see again. The Lord shall fight for you. Be still."

The pillar of fire and pillar of cloud moved from in front to behind the Israelites. The two pillars stood between Israel and the Egyptian army. The pillar of cloud blocked all light from Pharaoh and his men so that they were in darkness.

Doing as the Lord commanded him, Moses raised his staff up into the air, stretching it out toward the

MOSES RAISED HIS STAFF UP INTO THE AIR

sea. Miriam stood still and listened. Suddenly, the sound of a powerful wind filled the air. She looked and saw that the Red Sea was being buffeted by a vigorous east wind. In utter amazement all Israel watched as the wind pushed the water back so that it was divided. The wind blew all through the night, drying up the bottom of the sea.

At Moses' signal, the Israelites moved forward onto the path in the sea. To the right and to the left, the water stood still like liquid walls. The people hurried through the miraculous passageway to the other side of the sea. Pharaoh chased after them. The Lord slowed down the army by making the wheels of their chariots fly off.

"Let's get out of here!" the chariot drivers and the soldiers cried out. "The Lord is fighting for the Israelites! Retreat!"

As Pharaoh's army turned around and fled back toward the shore of the Red Sea, the Lord commanded Moses to raise up his staff once again. Moses did as he was commanded, and the walls of

THE WATER STOOD STILL LIKE LIQUID WALLS

water came crashing down. The roaring water swiftly engulfed the Egyptians. In a matter of moments, Pharaoh's army was no more.

At the awesome sight of such a powerful deliverance, deep reverence for the Lord their God captured the hearts of the Hebrews. They knew without a doubt they could trust the Lord and His servant Moses.

Moses' heart overflowed with joy and he began to sing a song of praise to the Lord. All the people joined in the singing. Miriam the prophetess picked up a tambourine and began to dance and sing: "Sing to the Lord, for He has triumphed gloriously, the horse and rider He has thrown into the sea." All the women followed Miriam in a glad procession, playing their tambourines, dancing and singing for joy to the Lord.

After the joyous celebration, the Lord led the Israelites south toward the desert of Sinai. He provided water for the Israelites as they needed it

PHARAOH'S ARMY WAS NO MORE

and a special food called manna. The manna fell to the ground every morning like a fine flour. The people gathered up the manna and made cakes with it. Also, as they traveled, their clothes and their sandals did not wear out.

It took the Israelites three months to reach the desert of Sinai. When they arrived, they set up camp at the base of Mount Sinai. The Lord came to the mountain top and called to Moses to join him there. Moses climbed Mount Sinai, leaving the people at the foot of the barren mountain. Thunder and lightning punctuated the air. Thick smoke covered Mount Sinai and suddenly a loud trumpet blast sounded forth. The people trembled with fear. As the Lord descended to the top of the mountain, a tremor rumbled through it. The Lord God Almighty was meeting with Moses. When Moses spoke with Him, the Lord answered.

For forty days Moses stayed up on the mountain with the Lord. God gave Moses the Ten Commandments by which Israel was to live, as well as

MOSES CLIMBED MOUNT SINAI

rules for the priesthood and directions for building the tabernacle for the Lord. Moses received two stone tablets on which the Lord had written His laws.

The days passed slowly for the Israelites. They became restless.

"Make us new gods!" they begged Aaron. "Moses has been gone so long! Maybe he isn't coming back. We will need new gods to lead us on our journey."

Aaron looked at the people. They were clamoring for a new god. Aaron felt he should do as they asked.

"Give me all your gold earrings," said Aaron.

The people did as he requested. Aaron took all the earrings and melted the gold. Then he made a god in the shape of a calf, like the golden calves worshipped in Egypt.

The people pointed to the calf. "Here is your god, O Israel, who brought you out of Egypt!"

When Aaron saw that the people revered their

HE MADE A GOD IN THE SHAPE OF A CALF

new god, he built an altar for the golden calf. "Tomorrow we will hold a festival in honor of the Lord," he announced, nodding toward the calf. The feeling of power burned through Aaron's veins. At last he was the one in charge, not his younger brother Moses!

Miriam remained silent. This couldn't be happening!

The next day the people brought sacrifices to the altar of the golden calf and worshiped it. Then they broke loose into a riotous celebration, doing whatever they felt like doing, right or wrong.

At the end of the forty days, the Lord told Moses to go down from the mountain. "These people you brought out of Egypt have been quick to abandon their faith in Me. They have made a golden calf their new god. Now leave Me alone, so I may bring My wrath against them and destroy them. And I will destroy your brother Aaron as well. Then I will make a nation come forth from you, Moses."

Moses pleaded for the Lord to be merciful.

MIRIAM REMAINED SILENT

"Remember Your promise to Abraham, Isaac, and Jacob? You must keep your promise to make them a nation and give them their own land. Besides, if You destroy the people, the Egyptians will say You brought Israel out in order to kill them!" Moses interceded for the Israelites. "And please, show Your mercy to my brother Aaron. Do not destroy him."

The Lord listened to Moses and decided not to destroy all of Israel. Moses left the top of the mountain, carrying the two tablets of stone. When he neared the camp and saw the calf and the celebration in full swing, anger welled up in Moses like a fire. In anger he threw the stone tablets to the ground, breaking them to pieces. The people stopped their dancing and watched in fear as Moses destroyed the golden calf.

Turning to Aaron, Moses demanded an explanation. "What did the people do to you, that you could bring so great a sin on them?"

Aaron begged Moses not to be angry. "You

ANGER WELLED UP IN MOSES LIKE A FIRE

yourself know how these people can so easily turn to do evil. They thought you weren't coming back, so they asked me to make them a god. I took the gold they gave me," Aaron lied, "and threw it into the fire. And out of the fire came this calf!"

Moses looked at the chaos of the camp and turned to stand at the gate. "Who is on the Lord's side? Come and stand by me." All the men of the tribe of Levi joined Moses. The Lord brought judgment on those who rejected Him. Many were slain that day in the camp of Israel.

Meeting with the Lord again, Moses received new tablets of stone with the commandments written on them. The Lord revealed His glory to Moses, and spoke to him as a man would speak to a friend. Moses came back down the mountain and gave the commandments to the people. This time they were ready to receive the Lord's commandments.

Moses instructed them to build a tabernacle for

THIS TIME THEY WERE READY...

the Lord. It was to be built according to the specifications that God had given to Moses. The people gladly gave the materials and skills needed to construct the tabernacle. After it was completed, Moses surveyed their work. The people had done everything the Lord had commanded them to do.

"The Lord bless you for being obedient to the Lord your God," said Moses to the people. "This is the Tent of Meeting for the Lord."

The pillar of cloud enveloped the Tent of Meeting and the glory of the Lord filled the inside of the tent. When the Lord wanted the Israelites to move on, the cloud would move up from the tabernacle. If the cloud did not lift up from the tent, the Israelites would stay where they were camped. The pillar of cloud by day, and the fire by night, remained over the tabernacle throughout their journey. All Israel could see that the Lord God was their leader and their guide.

MOSES SURVEYED THEIR WORK

"WE ARE SICK OF THIS MANNA!"

12

Traveling through the wilderness on foot was difficult. At times the monotony of the journey overwhelmed the Israelites. The people began to complain about their circumstances. Sometimes they became obsessed with wanting more water. Instead of humbly asking the Lord for water, they would complain that Moses had brought them out to die in the desert. Time after time, the Israelites would grumble and complain. TIme after time, Moses would intercede for the people so that God would have mercy on them.

One day the Israelites stood at the entrance of their tents, wailing and crying. "We are sick of this manna!" they said. "Back in Egypt we had meat, fish, and vegetables to eat. Day in and day out, all we have to eat is manna cakes. We were better off in Egypt!"

Moses prayed to the Lord for help. The Lord sent

a wind that carried with it quail from the sea. There were so many quail that they were piled up three feet high in the camp. When the rebellious people gathered in the birds and prepared to cook and eat them, the judgment of the Lord fell on them. Those with the food in their mouths were struck down with a plague.

The quarreling and complaining in the camp was infectious. Even Miriam was getting tired of hearing about Moses. A spark of jealousy began to burn in her heart. She would watch Moses go to the Tent of Meeting. The cloud of the Lord would block the entrance so no one could enter while Moses was inside with the Lord.

Day after day Miriam's frustration grew. She watched as the people hung on Moses' every word. She watched as Moses went often to the Tent of Meeting and met with the Lord. The people were in awe of her brother. Moses gave the commandments of the Lord and the regulations

A SPARK OF JEALOUSLY BEGAN TO BURN IN HER HEART

concerning all the aspects of life for the Israelites.

When Moses married a woman from Ethiopia, that was the last straw for Miriam.

She hurried over to Aaron's tent, her face etched with anger and bitterness. She burst into his home, her eyes flashing.

"Why, Miriam, what is the matter?" Aaron asked with concern in his voice. "What happened?"

"I'll tell you what happened! That brother of ours has gone and married an Ethiopian woman. Can you imagine such a thing! She's not a Hebrew! He has no business marrying someone like that. She's not one of us." Miriam's words seethed with prejudice and jealousy. "I think it is an outrage."

Aaron took his sister by the hand and tried to calm her down.

"You mustn't get so upset, Miriam. Surely the woman reveres the Lord our God. Moses would not marry an unbeliever."

"I THINK IT IS AN OUTRAGE!"

"I don't care if she is a believer. She is not an Israelite. If Moses is such a great leader of Israel, shouldn't he marry only a Hebrew woman?"

Aaron stroked his beard thoughtfully. "Well, I guess so," he said slowly.

Miriam leaned forward toward her brother. "Aaron, is Moses the only one the Lord has spoken through? Hasn't he spoken through us as well? Hasn't the Lord spoken through you, Aaron, and through me?"

Her brother nodded. Her words stirred up rebellion in his own heart. "You're right, Miriam. Moses isn't the only leader in Israel! Why, we are leaders just as much as he is. He really shouldn't think so highly of himself."

The truth of the matter was that Moses was a very humble man. The moment Miriam and Aaron finished their poisonous conversation, they heard the voice of the Lord in the camp.

"Come to the Tent of Meeting at once," the Lord said to Moses, Aaron, and Miriam.

"...WE ARE LEADERS JUST AS MUCH AS HE IS"

MIRIAM

The two brothers and their sister made their way to the Tent of Meeting. Miriam's heart was pounding. She knew immediately she had been wrong to speak about her brother Moses the way she did.

They approached the Tent of Meeting and waited for the Lord. He came down to them in a pillar of cloud. Standing at the door of the Tent of Meeting, he called Aaron and Miriam to come forward. They obeyed. Miriam was trembling with fear.

"Listen to what I have to say," the Lord said. "If there is a prophet of the Lord in your midst, I speak to him through visions and dreams. The prophet interprets the symbols and meanings of the dreams and visions as I reveal them to him. But with Moses My servant, this is not the way I work. He is faithful to Me. I speak to him clearly, face to face, not in dreams and visions. He sees the form of the Lord. Since Moses shares such a special relationship with the Lord your God, why weren't you afraid to speak against My servant in this terrible way?"

MIRIAM WAS TREMBLING WITH FEAR

MIRIAM

The Lord was angry with Aaron and Miriam and he left the Tent of Meeting. Aaron hung his head in shame. Suddenly he heard Miriam cry out in anguish. Aaron looked at his sister. To his horror, she was completely white with leprosy.

Miriam suddenly felt weak. She held up her hands in front of her face. They were pale and lifeless. Tears streamed down her face as she saw that the Lord had brought judgment upon her. It would only be a matter of time before the disease began to deform her body and eventually take her life.

Aaron turned back toward Moses and called to him. "O my lord," he spoke fervently and with genuine respect for his brother, "I beg you not to hold this sin against us. We have been foolish." He pointed to Miriam, his voice breaking with love and sorrow. "Do not let her be like this, her body being ravaged and destroyed."

Moses cried out to the Lord for his sister. "Heal her now, O Lord, I beseech You."

"HEAL HER NOW, O LORD, I BESEECH YOU"

The Lord answered Moses and healed her. "She must be ashamed of what she has done," the Lord said to Moses. "You must shut her out of the camp for seven days. After that, she can be received into the camp again."

Moses, Aaron, and Miriam left the Tent of Meeting. Aaron helped Miriam with a water bag and a basket of food. Aaron wept as he lead his sister out of the camp. Miriam, overcome with sorrow and remorse, couldn't speak.

"I'll come and get you in seven days," Aaron said softly to Miriam. "Don't be afraid."

Miriam nodded and watched her brother as he turned and walked back into the camp. A wave of loneliness swept over her. She laid her mat down in the shadow of a bush and fell on it, weeping.

How could I have done such a thing? she thought to herself. The words of her father Amram came to her again. "You are all special to the Lord. His hand is on you and Aaron and Moses."

"After all that the Lord has done through Moses,

"...HOW COULD I SPEAK AGAINST HIM?"

how could I speak against him?" she sobbed. Her tears were bitter.

As Miriam wept, night began to fall. Through her tears, she could see the pillar of fire shining its wondrous light on the Hebrew camp. She finally stopped crying and sat up. The light from the fire dispelled the darkness around the camp. Miriam gratefully soaked in the warmth from the huge pillar. She pulled her cloak tightly around her shoulders.

"O Lord, forgive me," she prayed. "I was so jealous of Moses. I won't ever speak another unkind word about him, or any of Your servants." She sighed and looked over at the camp. "Let me serve You in the path You have chosen for me, Lord. Let me not try to walk someone else's path."

Miriam fell asleep, under the stars and beneath the light of God's presence. For seven days she prayed and sat quietly, waiting for the day she would be received back into the camp. The Israelites were not to move on until Miriam was

"O LORD, FORGIVE ME"

restored to them.

At daybreak on the seventh day, Miriam awoke and looked up. She saw her brother Aaron hurrying toward her.

"Miriam!" cried Aaron. He looked her over carefully. "As high priest of the Lord, I pronounce you clean of leprosy. You can return to the camp," he said happily. "Come with me, my sister."

He reached out his hand. Miriam whispered a prayer of thanks and put her hand in his. Together they returned to the camp.

"COME WITH ME, MY SISTER"

"WE CAN TAKE THE LAND"

13

The day finally arrived when the Israelites reached the borders of Canaan, the Promised Land. Moses sent twelve spies to explore the land and report their findings. They returned with mixed feelings.

"The land is just as the Lord promised! It is flowing with milk and honey!" said the spies. "But the people who inhabit the land are too strong for us. We would never be able to drive them out. There are even giants in the land!"

Two of the spies, Joshua and Caleb, didn't agree with the other men. "We can take the land," said Caleb, full of faith. "I know we can do it."

The fearful spies would not listen to Joshua and Caleb. They spread their fear throughout the camp until all the Israelites were quaking and crying with fright. Miriam and those who trusted the

Lord tried to calm the people down. But no one would listen.

"We are all going to be killed by the giants!" cried the people. "We need a new leader who will take us back to Egypt!"

Moses and Aaron fell on their faces in anguish. Caleb and Joshua called out to the people above the weeping and grumbling. "We can take the land!" they said. "The Lord will help us!"

"I say we stone all four of them!" someone shouted from the crowd.

"Yeah! Let's stone them!" others shouted as the crowd's anger and rebelliousness grew.

Suddenly, the glory of the Lord appeared at the tabernacle.

"How long will these people rebel against Me? Why will they not believe in Me, after all the miracles I have performed on their behalf? I should destroy them and make a nation out of you."

Moses again pleaded for mercy. "You must

"LET'S STONE THEM!"

show Egypt that You can do as You promised. You promised to bring these people to this land. And You told me yourself on Mount Sinai that You are filled with love and forgiveness. Please forgive these people for this sin."

The Lord listened to Moses and forgave the people. But the spies who spread fear throughout the camp were struck down with a plague.

A man named Korah, who was of the tribe of Levi, gathered together three other men. "I've had enough of this Moses. It's time we did something about him."

So Korah, Dathan, Abiram, and On rallied two hundred and fifty men to confront Moses and Aaron. These men were all leaders in the camp, familiar to all the people. Together they marched up to Moses and Aaron. "Who do you think you are?" they demanded with a sneer. "You think you are the only holy ones in the camp? All of us are holy, not just you and Aaron!"

Miriam stood with the leaders who supported Moses and Aaron. Her heart broke at the sight of such rebellion. It reminded her of her own rebellion, when she had tried to put herself in Moses' place. Miriam silently cried out to the Lord in her heart. "Help us, Lord. Help Moses and Aaron!" Moses stood up to the men.

"It is not against us that you are grumbling. The Lord has appointed Aaron high priest. So it is against the Lord you are rebelling! Dathan and Abiram, come up here!" Moses called for the two men.

"We will not come," the men replied. "You took us out of Egypt, a land of plenty, and brought us to the desert to die. Will you make slaves of us as well?"

At those words, Moses became angry. "Tomorrow the Lord will deal with you. You will see whom the Lord has chosen to be priest, Aaron or you."

The next day Israel gathered to see what was

"... THE LORD WILL DEAL WITH YOU"

going to happen

"Move away from the tents of these wicked men!" said Moses.

The people moved away from the tents. Suddenly the ground split open and devoured Korah and his cohorts. A fire broke forth and destroyed the two hundred and fifty men who had supported Korah.

Miriam returned to her tent, grateful that Moses and Aaron were safe. As she sat on her mat and stirred the coals in her little oven, she treasured the promises of God in her heart. Thoughts of her mother's faith brought a smile to her face. "Yes, Jochebed," she said softly. "The Lord is truly glorious!"

The Israelites travelled on and in the first month arrived at a place known as Kadesh. Miriam was very old and she knew her time had come to die. Moses and Aaron came to see her and she said goodbye to them. She took them by the hand and a shy smile lit up her face. " 'Kadesh' means

THE GROUND SPLIT OPEN

holy," she whispered. "How good the Lord is to let me die in a holy place!   Surely the Lord is abounding with love and forgiveness."

Miriam died at Kadesh and they buried her on a mountain in that holy place.

THEY BURIED HER ON A MOUNTAIN IN THAT HOLY PLACE

MIRIAM WAS A WOMAN WHO SERVED THE LORD

EPILOGUE

Miriam was a woman who served the Lord. The Lord used her to help protect the life of the baby who would become the deliverer of Israel. She was called a prophetess, one who hears from God. Despite her faults and her rebellion, it is clear in the Scriptures that Miriam was a vital figure in the history of Israel.

Another woman in history had a name that was derived from the name Miriam. Her name was Mary, the mother of the baby who would become our deliverer from sin, Jesus Christ.

More than seven hundred years after her death, Miriam is spoken of in the Scriptures, her name linked with the names of her brothers: "I have brought you up out of Egypt [says the Lord] and

redeemed you from the land of slavery. I sent Moses to lead you also, Aaron and Miriam."
(*Micah 6:4,* New International Version)

GLOSSARY

bitumen— a semisolid dark substance; asphalt

hyssop— a leafy plant used for dipping and sprinkling liquids

leeks— an onion like vegetable

locusts— an insect similar to a grasshopper but larger and migratory

unleavened bread— bread made without leaven that does not rise and therefore is flat

Awesome

Books
for Kids!